Dear Parents / Teachers:

Thank you for buying the third book in the **M is for Money**™ series. I hope you enjoyed **The Little Piggy Bank** and **The Little Lemonade Stand**.

M is for Money™ is a Kid's Guide to Financial Literacy™. It is a chance for you to explain the rudimentary facts about money to your children and students.

Book 3, The Little Trip to the Bank, continues with the financial adventures of our main characters - Tessa and Benji.

Tessa and Benji open bank accounts, learn that the bank will keep their money safe on their behalf and are reassured that they can take their money out of the bank whenever they need it.

If you haven't already done so, perhaps this is a good time for you to bring your child to a bank and open an account for him or her.

I hope this book and the others in the series give you and your children and students the opportunity to enjoy many conversations about money.

Tessa and Benji's trip to the big, big piggy bank with their little piggy banks awaits. Read on!

—Teresa

Tessa & Benji **a kid's guide to financial literacy**™ books follow the financial adventures of twin siblings & . They introduce children to the concept of money, its use and value, as well as its charitable capabilities.

*Visit **www.MisforMoney.ca**
for fun facts and to order
Tessa and Benji play items!*

Tessa & Benji a kid's guide to financial literacy ™

M is for Money™
The Little Trip to the Bank
The Big, Big Piggy Bank

Created & Written by
Teresa Cascioli

Illustrations by
Rachel Zavarella

Published in Canada by Tess Creative™, Ontario, Canada, 2015.

All ™ trademarks are owned by Tess Creative™.

This book is a work of fiction. Names, characters, places and incidents either are the product of the author's and/or illustrator's imagination or are used fictitiously. Any resemblance to actual persons, living or dead, event or locales is entirely coincidental.

Library and Archives Canada Cataloguing in Publication

Cascioli, Teresa, 1961-, author
    The little trip to the bank / created & written by Teresa Cascioli
; illustrated by Rachel Zavarella.

(M is for money ; book 3)
Issued in print and electronic formats.
ISBN 978-1-987905-02-1 (pbk.).--ISBN 978-1-987905-23-6 (ebook)

    1. Finance, Personal--Juvenile literature. 2. Money--Juvenile
literature. I. Zavarella, Rachel, illustrator II. Title. III. Series: Cascioli,
Teresa, 1961- . M is for money ; bk. 3.

HG179.C383 bk. 3 2015   j332.024   C2015-900701-1
                                                 C2015-902163-4

ISBN: 978-1-987905-02-1

Visit us at www.MisforMoney.ca for further fun information on the characters and other interesting facts.

Printed and bound in Canada. First edition.

Cover design and illustration by Rachel Zavarella.

Teresa Cascioli & Rachel Zavarella support and celebrate the freedom of thought.

Published by Tess Creative™

www.MisforMoney.ca
Cover art by Rachel Zavarella

To My Mrs. Chan

A long time ago,
a coin I would save,
for a time in the future,
for roads to be paved.

I scrimped,
and I struggled
but a coin I did save.

My banker would smile.
"You'll be ready for rain."

Hello, everyone. My name is Tessa and this is my brother, Benji. We are twins.

Today we are taking a trip to a special place. Let me tell you about it in this story.

Benji and I each have a piggy bank.

The other day we were playing with our piggy banks and jiggling them around. We noticed that they were a little heavy.

Every time we get some coins or bills, we put them in our piggy bank.

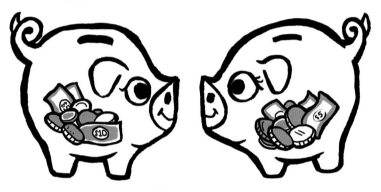

We earn money when we do chores. Mom and Dad give us coins each time.

Nickel
5¢

Quarter
25¢

Dime
10¢

Loonie
$1

Toonie
$2

On our birthday our family gave us paper money as a present. We can use it to buy whatever we like.

Ten-dollar bill

Five-dollar bill

We received even more coins when we set up a lemonade stand at the end of our driveway on a very hot day. Each time we gave our neighbours cups of lemonade, they gave us coins in return.

"Mom, we put all of our money in our piggy banks," said Benji. "Now I think our piggy banks are getting full."

"What will we do if we get more money and it won't fit inside their bellies?" I asked.

"Should we use the money to buy something?" Benji asked. "The piggy banks won't have as much money inside if we do."

"Well, let's start by seeing how much money you have in your piggy banks," Mom said.

Benji and I opened the stoppers at the bottom of the piggy banks and out came our coins and our paper money.

"Wow, there is a lot of money here, Tessa!" said Benji.

We separated all of our coins and paper money and then Mom helped us count it.

"You each have 26 dollars and 15 cents here. **Dollars** and **cents** is the name for your paper and coin money when you add it up," said Mom.

This is how much money we each had in our piggy bank:

(1)

1 Loonie 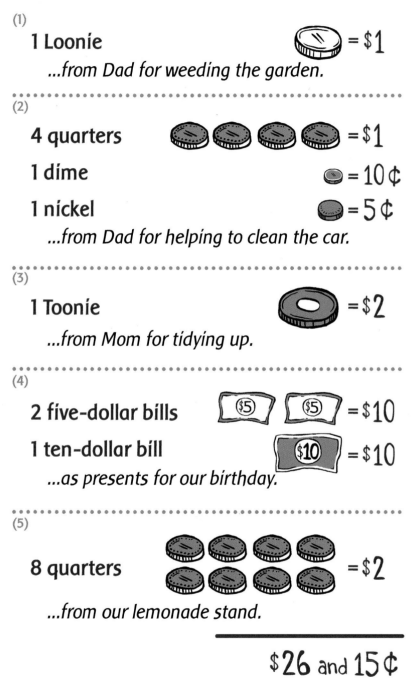 = $1

...from Dad for weeding the garden.

(2)

4 quarters = $1

1 dime = 10¢

1 nickel = 5¢

...from Dad for helping to clean the car.

(3)

1 Toonie = $2

...from Mom for tidying up.

(4)

2 five-dollar bills = $10

1 ten-dollar bill = $10

...as presents for our birthday.

(5)

8 quarters = $2

...from our lemonade stand.

$26 and 15¢

Total: $26.15

(1) Book 1, Page 11. (2) Book 1, Page 17. (3) Book 1, Page 23. (4) Book 1, Pages 29 and 31. (5) Book 2, Page 23.

"Do either of you want to buy anything?" asked Mom.

Benji and I looked at each other. We were not sure what we could buy because we had all of the toys we wanted.

"I don't really want or need anything, Mom," said Benji.

"How about you, Tessa? Do you need anything?" Mom asked.

"No, not really," I replied.

"If you don't need anything now, it's best to save your money until there is something important to spend it on," Mom said.

"Let's put your money in a place called the bank. Your money will be safe there. You can take it out of the bank any time you want," she said.

"After you put your money in the bank, your piggy banks will be empty. You can begin to fill them again as you receive or earn more money," Mom explained.

14

"Is the bank like a big, big piggy bank?" I asked.

"Yes, Tessa." Mom chuckled. "We can visit the bank tomorrow and you can see it for yourself."

The next morning, Benji and I were excited about taking our piggy banks full of our money to the bank.

When we arrived, a woman at the counter asked us for our names. She said her name was Mrs. Chan.

We emptied our piggy banks for Mrs. Chan. She said she would set up a **bank account** for each of us.

"The bank will take care of your money for you until you need it," said Mrs. Chan.

Mrs. Chan gave us each a piece of paper with our name on it. The paper showed exactly how much each of us had in our bank account.

"Your bank account can grow or shrink," said Mrs. Chan.

"If you bring more money to the bank, your account will grow. If you take money out of the bank to buy something special, your account will shrink," she explained.

"Thanks, Mrs. Chan. We are happy that our piggy banks are empty. Now when we do more chores, receive money as a special gift or sell more lemonade, we will have a place to keep our money again," I said.

"Yes, and when your piggy banks are full again, you can bring them here and put the money in your new bank accounts," said Mrs. Chan.

On our way home, Benji and I began to think of ways that we could add more coins or paper money to our piggy banks.

"Mom, do you have any chores for us to do?" we asked.

"You could help me fold the laundry," she said.

"What else, Mom? What else?" we asked.

"There are many chores that need to be done, you two! Little by little, your piggy banks will begin to fill up once more," Mom said.

"Just think, Benji, before we know it we will be visiting Mrs. Chan again," I said.

"Not so fast, Tessa," Benji said. "I am not going to bring all of my money to Mrs. Chan. I want to spend some of my money. I am going to think of something special that I want to buy."

"Cousin Sophie's birthday is coming. Maybe you can buy her a present," I said.

When we got home, we ran inside with our empty piggy banks. Dad was waiting in the kitchen.

"Hello there. Did you two enjoy your time at the bank?" Dad asked.

"Yes, Dad," we replied. "We each have a bank account. We can add more money or take it out any time we like."

Today we met Mrs. Chan. She works at the bank. The bank is like a big, big piggy bank. Now that our piggy banks are empty we can think of fun ways to fill their bellies.

To download the
Tessa & Benji
M is for Money™ song,

Nickels & Dimes©

visit our website at
www.MisforMoney.ca

Look & Find Game

Book 3
Can you find these things in the story?
Good Luck!

10 Toonie Coins

5 Question Marks

9 Ten-Dollar Bills

4 Sunshine Faces

8 Tulip Flowers

3 Bank Buildings

7 Puzzle Pieces

2 Lemons

6 Stoppers for Piggy Banks

1 Flower Vase

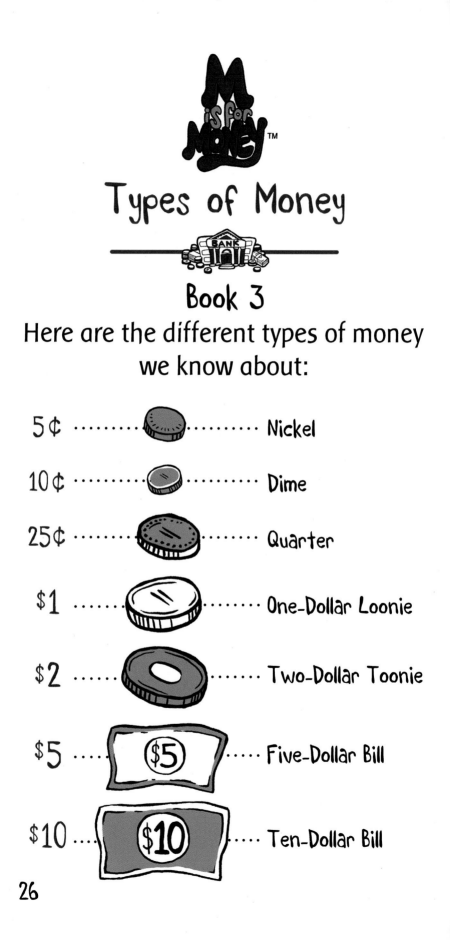

Types of Money

Book 3

Here are the different types of money we know about:

5¢ ·········· **Nickel**

10¢ ·········· **Dime**

25¢ ·········· **Quarter**

$1 ·········· **One-Dollar Loonie**

$2 ·········· **Two-Dollar Toonie**

$5 ·········· **Five-Dollar Bill**

$10 ·········· **Ten-Dollar Bill**

The Money Tree

Book 3
How We Get Money

We earn or receive money from...

Chores   Gifts   Lemonade Stand

When we have money we can...

Keep it in our piggy banks   Buy gifts

Take it to the bank   Use it to buy special things

BANK

Our Family

Can you fill in the blanks with the names of our family?

The ♥ shows you our family members who are married.

Our Friends

Can you fill in the blanks with the names of our friends?

Mrs. Morris

Mr. Duncan

Holly

Tessa

Age 7, has a twin brother named Benji

Loves: Hair bows for her pigtails, crayons, books and dolls

Best Friend: Her cousin Sophie

Mom and Dad

Parents to Tessa and Benji

Mom Loves: Cooking, reading and hiking

Dad Loves: Gardening, driving his car and watching hockey

Aunt Rose and Uncle Sam

Parents to Freddy and Sophie

Aunt Rose Loves: Volunteering at the school, hiking and reading

Uncle Sam Loves: Making pizza, watching soccer and riding his bike

Freddy

Age 5, has a sister named Sophie

Loves: Toy trucks, building blocks and storybooks

Best Friend: His cousin Benji

Mrs. Morris and Holly

Live across the street from Tessa and Benji

Mrs. Morris Loves: Gardening and sailing

Holly Loves: Chew toys and cheese

Benji

Age 7, has a twin sister named Tessa

Loves: Bow ties, toy cars and puzzles
Best Friend: His cousin Freddy

Grandma and Grandpa

Parents to Mom and Aunt Rose

Love: Visiting their grandchildren
Grandma Loves: Knitting and making Christmas ornaments
Grandpa Loves: Woodworking and playing cards

Sophie

Age 7, has a brother named Freddy and recently lost a tooth

Loves: Chocolate cake, ballet and piano lessons
Best Friend: Her cousin Tessa

Mr. Duncan and Rufus

Live next door to Tessa and Benji

Mr. Duncan Loves: Lemonade and baseball
Rufus Loves: Dog bones and peanut butter

Mr. Nichols

Lives two doors down from Tessa and Benji

Loves: Cooking, volunteering at the local hospital and painting

Mrs. Chan

Works at the bank where she keeps Tessa and Benji's money safe

Loves: Chess, photography and skiing

My Bank Account

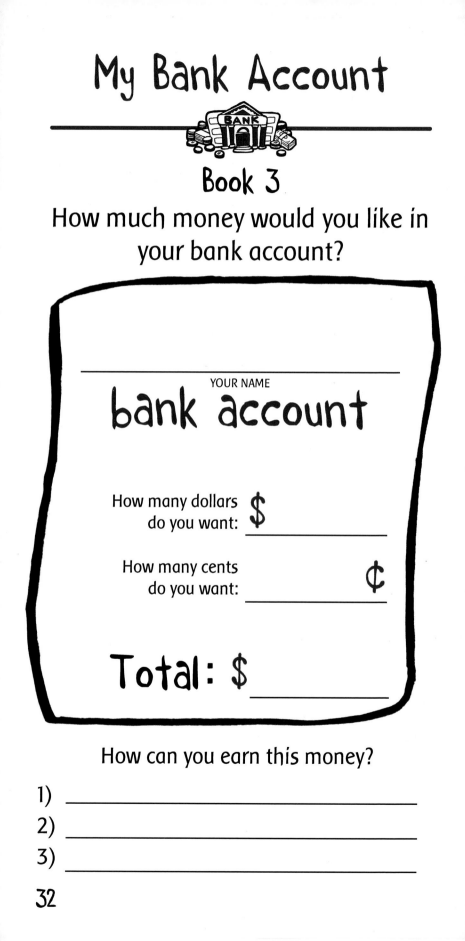

Book 3

How much money would you like in your bank account?

_____
YOUR NAME

bank account

How many dollars
do you want: **$** _____

How many cents
do you want: _____ **¢**

Total: $ _____

How can you earn this money?

1) _____

2) _____

3) _____

M is for Money™ Award

TO

FOR

Reading the first three books in the
M is for Money™ Book Series.

_____   _____
Presented By   Date

Fun & Games

Book 3

Visit **www.MisforMoney.ca** for Tessa and Benji play items from their trip to the bank and other adventures!

Tessa Ten-Dollar Play Bills

Benji Five-Dollar Play Bills

More Fun Stuff

Reward Sticky Notes

Jumbo Magnets

Colouring Book

Bookmarks

Stickers

Birthday Cards and Party Invitations

Lemonade Sign with Recipe Card

About the Author & Creator of
Tessa & Benji - a Kid's Guide to Financial Literacy™
M is for Money™

Teresa Cascioli

Teresa Cascioli is one of Canada's top business minds. She is the daughter of Italian immigrants and a Commerce graduate of McMaster University in Hamilton, Ontario.

As the former CEO of Lakeport Brewing she took the company from bankruptcy to a $201 million sale to Labatt in just eight years. She lead one of the country's most successful income trust public offerings. This award-winning entrepreneur has been featured on *Profit* and *Chatelaine Magazine*'s lists of Canada's most successful women and has been named one of the Women's Executive Network *Top 100 Canada's Most Powerful Women*. She was awarded *Entrepreneur of the Year* by Canada's Venture Capital and Private Equity Association as well as by Ernst & Young in their Turnaround Category. She was inducted in the Sales Hall of Fame by the Canadian Professional Sales Association. In 2012, Cascioli was awarded the Queen's Diamond Jubilee Medal.

Teresa served as Strategic Advisor to Labatt and KPMG. Today, she devotes her spare time to charitable causes. She has donated in excess of $6 million to her community, including the funding of McMaster University's Chair in Entrepreneurial Leadership. Her charitable leadership earned her the title of *Philanthropist of the Year* in her community. Teresa lives in Halton Region, Ontario.

About the Illustrator

Rachel Zavarella

Rachel Zavarella is an illustrator from Ontario, Canada. She is a 2014 Honours graduate of the Bachelor of Applied Arts Illustration Program at Sheridan College in Ontario. She was the sole graduate to be awarded the prestigious *Canon Award of Merit* from the Sheridan Illustration Graduate Art Show for her thesis presentation.